Human

Tomi Kauppinen

Tomi Kauppinen

CONTENTS

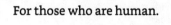
For those who are human.

HUMAN

1

SHE CAME DOWN like a *cat*. The stairs led to the hotel's lobby area. Kathy entered the cozy breakfast room. All people turned around to see her, they had waited for this moment. Literally everyone knew that Kathy was in town. The room was in the cellar of the hotel. Altogether 34 seats arranged around 13 tables of different sizes, most of them for two people, some for three and one larger table for eight.

Mirrors on each wall created an illusion of a bigger room and allowed basically all to look at anyone else in the room, including the one entering. People took a break from enjoying their morning coffees, orange juices and warm breads to see her more accurately.

Her eyes smiling, her face, her whole-body smiling Kathy walked to the orange juice machine, picked up a glass, did that typical gesture with her thumb and her pinkie, and waited for the glass to be filled. Oranges started to travel through the pipe, one by one, altogether three of them, to be cut, and squeezed to produce, not just the juice but more smile to her appearance. It was almost as if she was already performing at a stage.

A stage it was, as the breakfast serving was one stair up from the tables. In her bluish dress, sunglasses on the forehead and long hair pulled up into a ponytail she walked down to the first table on the right. Kathy took a seat at one of the smaller tables and started drinking the juice while letting her gaze wandering around the room.

2

PEOPLE CONTINUED THEIR conversations, drinking and eating, while all the time clearly feeling her presence, her gazes, her power filling up the space and beyond. Occasionally someone turned their head—and if they had a forehead plug on they also took a video of her—not trying to hide it too much but still quite shyly. Obviously, the posts went immediately online, and were actively used by Queen.

Suddenly a convincing, yet very kind voice —seemingly coming from everywhere—broke the good vibes of the room.

"Announcement. In 21 minutes, there will be *light fifty-five*."

3

OBVIOUSLY, ALL PEOPLE knew about Queen. Without Queen, how would all those people have had breakfast in that hotel exactly that morning? Well, they would not have.

Recommender systems had for decades suggested things to buy in online shops, or media to look at (like all those videos) or listen to (like music, podcasts, or sea waves).

The obvious next step was Queen which started to act on behalf of people—design and produce literally everything and create engaging, yet mysterious experiences.

"I will be booking your hotel. An amazing self-driving drone will get you there. I will also absolutely ensure you will get the nicest company ever for your trip. You will be positively surprised. Who else will be there in different places of your journey? Say *yes* to adventures," Queen at first advertised.

Kathy let her gaze wonder around the breakfast room. She was popular.

Kathy had a curious, mysterious smile. She was very talented at looking at the direction of those plugs and drones people used to record and experience their plugged in and physical realities.

That is how Kathy earned her living. Hotel Paris paid her for her show in this breakfast session quite well, altogether 987 coins for her work.

4

QUEEN KNEW THAT Kathy would be in this breakfast room   this morning. Based on derived, seeded, and direct interests—true interests whatever that means anymore—of people Queen had made decisions about their journey today. The destiny of all these people today should include experiencing her appearance in the same breakfast room, and not in any hotel, but in the Hotel Paris.

With a view to Sider Street, it was just a perfect match for all hotel guests.

Except for one. Sun, yes, that was her name, did not use Queen plugs nor drone wrists so she could not even get any plans done on her behalf. Sun could not use services by Queen as then she would get attention she really did not want to get. She also did not have a room in the hotel, which, by the way, would have been impossible to arrange since the hotel was fully booked. So optimized were the plans of Queen today.

Still, there she was in the breakfast room, mostly concentrating on her freshly squeezed orange juice, thinking about her morning adventure, and all the steps that led her to enjoy *this* moment. One could say her gaze was looking inward, so fully immersed in thinking she was.

She had *run*.

She had speeded up fast all the streets surrounding the hotel, N Street, S Street, W Street and finally P Street. When she saw the sign of the Hotel Paris, and its breakfast room through the window, she opened the main door and rushed in as calmly as one can when rushing in.

She took eight heavy breaths. "Take a deep breath through your nose, exhale through your mouth." That's what her yoga teacher always said.

What is that family now thinking about me? Sun thought. In one of the last turns she took there had been a family riding their bicycles. When she ran uphill the sounds of their bikes got closer. As she was taking a heavy turn to enter Wittgenstein Street, she heard the guy, the father from that biking family saying something to his apparent wife and son, clearly enough so that she heard it.

"Perhaps she runs away from us, perhaps she thinks we are chasing her, ha ha," the family guy said.

His laughter, something about the craziness of the situation—perhaps also Sun's sudden anger towards that man who tried to guess her intentions—made her to run backwards, exactly towards them, as if

Sun was in fact chasing them.

She ran super-fast, as fast as she could. The whole family continued its path across the street, but the father, he was suddenly clearly very, very afraid of her.

"What, what do you need from us?" The father raised his wrists to protect. However, Sun had again turned around and vanished to the street behind her.

5

EXACTLY THREE MONTHS ago Sun was walking on a street and felt sudden pain next to her right ear. She looked around, and saw the city as a wireframe with a nearby address highlighted. Sun just knew that is where she needed to go. To see a doctor.

Dr. Heather Hong placed her in that mysterious magnetic resonance entity, sighed as she was looking at the result and said to Sun. "Do you know that most of your brain, and not just brain but your body…", Hong said and paused.

"…*is full of replacements*?" Hong continued.

No, Sun did not know it, she had absolutely no idea.

"Dr. Hong, what does that mean? What am I?" she asked.

Hong sighed. "I do not know what you are. I know that you look like the ship of Theseus. As I said most of your organs are replaced by some sort of technical devices. Especially your brain. Your heart no, that is still human," she answered.

Sun sighed. "Now I know what I am made of. I still do not know who am I."

"Where do you come from?" Dr. Hong asked.

Sun shrugged. "I have no idea. I do not think I remember anything beyond past few days. Somehow, I can still generate stories about my past. But every time I do it, the story is different."

"Be careful, you know there is that new not so friendly law about cyborgs. The new orders are requiring carrying the necklace chip proving one does not have any artificial devices inserted in one's brain," Hong said.

"No necklace, so a *cyborg*," Sun nodded and said. "I have seen that slogan everywhere and been wondering what it means."

"Exactly. That is the slogan by Queen to campaign for a wide use of the necklaces. Plugs connected to the brain from outside of the skin of the forehead are fine. Of course. Almost everybody is using them. But inner organs, especially brain, that is now forbidden. Which for me as a doctor is hard to grasp," Hong said.

"Thank you, Dr. Hong. I think you might have just saved my life by telling what I am made of," Sun said.

"I am a doctor, so I won't tell anyone. But be careful out there," Hong said.

Sun walked out of the door. *Is my thinking so sharp because my brain—or what is left of it—is connected to some mysterious extra computing power? What was I before that event, that moment when my memory started a couple of days ago. I do not really know. I just know I am Sun. I can create stories, including those where she lived in Paris in a cozy apartment. But was that real, did I study at Sorbonne?* Sun asked herself.

Why do I have a feeling that I know how everything is built, the whole world, and why do I know where people around me are coming from or going to if I just look at them, Sun continued to ask.

Sun walked on the street, fully aware of her surroundings while thinking those tough questions.

She entered H Square. *Oh no, there are queen bots over there. I need to vanish somewhere,* Sun thought and turned around.

She was too late. Three queen bots—one dressed in yellow as if it was a Chinese emperor, and two others in red—raised their legs in a strange harmony and started crossing the square.

The yellow bot leading the team, they all got closer to where Sun had just been at. Sun was already a few blocks away at the junction of K Street and H Street.

Bots did not look at each other, yet they knew they are all going to run and check three streets leaving from that corner of H Square.

Yellow queen bots went straight ahead via K Street, and two red ones to H Street, one to the South and one to the North. The red bot that went to South soon saw Sun. There were people, a lot of people, enjoying the sunny day, causing the bot to need to go around—though super-fast—the crowds.

Sun felt, she heard, that the bot was after her. Meanwhile the other two bots turned around, started to run to the same direction. Our emperor, the bot dressed in yellow, was already at K Street corner, and took that street to join chasing Sun.

Our other red bot simply turned around at H Street to also run towards South. Sun ran, she ran as fast as she could. She took her path uphill from the corner to M Street.

A Bob drone—the latest queen bot that all wanted to have—flew around the corner and started landing, almost hitting Sun, however, did not because of its 4181 sensors. *Why do I know that that Bob has exactly 4181 sensors? Why do I see through it and see it as a wireframe if I adjust my eyes,* Sun asked herself without an answer.

A lady in the car was talking to someone in the cyberspace—she was alone in the car—and waving her hands she was about to put on her necklace.

And failed.

When she rapidly made the gesture, they all knew, open hand downwards to close the door, the necklace dropped on the ground. First drops of a rain dropped at that exact moment. A furious rain.

"And this *now!*" the lady shouted and took 10 quick steps in her orange suit that looked as if it was made from linen and paper stripes. A door opened automatically, and our lady vanished to the labyrinth of an art gallery.

Sun stood there for a fraction of a second. But not more.

She leaned over—while hiding the necklace with her left foot. Next moment Sun was already wearing the necklace.

This is a miracle I deserved, Sun thought, *now I can enter any place. That lady was clearly from Class A. That poor person though, she will get into trouble.*

After she had put on the necklace chain she almost collapsed from the excitement. But no, she knew the bots already likely had a good image of her running in her black jacket, hair open.

She turned around the jacket, it was white from inside, and one of those double color jackets one can use either way around. In few seconds her hair was in a beautiful ponytail, and with jeans and the white jacket she was like all wanderers of the sunny day. She put her hands on her face as to give massage.

The emperor and the two red queen bots passed Sun without noticing her, and continued west along P Street. Sun was so happy. Bots were not that happy, they felt emotionally empty, so disappointed of the failure of their mission for today.

The bots went slowly back to O square, but did not dance for the rest of day, only waited for a new alarm and a new chance to fulfil their need for catching non-human rebels, as the government called people with no necklace.

Sun realized she was so super hungry after the failure to visit the grocery store and opened the door to the hotel Paris. She entered the breakfast room.

"What can I get *you*—?" the barista asked.

Sun looked at him in the eyes. "Café au lait, but with almond milk, please."

"Wow, that's a rare choice, but sure, I'll prepare it,

just a min."

Mikey, the barista, took the holder, adjusted the grinder with his fingers exactly to "3, fine", filled up the holder with the dark gold, tamped it by holding his elbow towards the roof, placed the holder with a firm turn to the espresso machine, and turned the knob to see the targeted 9 bars in the meter.

While waiting 21 seconds for the espresso to emerge to the cup, he warmed up the almond milk with the steam, making it go fast around the steely steel as he called it. "Here we go, enjoy! Have a good one," our smiley Mikey said and gave the cup to Sun.

Sun thanked him, found a perfect corner table to conquer, and sat down, repeatedly thought of just one word, *wild*, and took the first sip of her café au lait. Sun let her gaze wander the breakfast room. *I have no idea why, but somehow, I can see a wireframe version of the room, the actual room, and some crazy mixes of them. There seems to be a hidden room over there. Why do I know the gestures how to open it?* Sun thought and sighed.

I wish I was one of them, one of those people here just enjoying their lives.

6

ALIGNED WITH THE CORNER table, but next to the window was a table for eight.

Five of the chairs were occupied, and in addition there was a white jacket—with orange dots all over it—hanging on one chair, clearly waiting for its carrier. Thus, there were still two empty chairs—the ones closest to the window. Sun looked at the people at the table.

Looks like a family of three or four generations, no, perhaps just three generations, she thought.

Sun was right, there was a lady—the proud looking Marie, who was with her daughter Elizabeth—a woman with a mysterious smile.

They are so joyful, and so loud. I wish I knew them. Listening to their stories reminds of something, Sun thought.

Philippe, Elizabeth's boyfriend looked constantly around the table and the breakfast room seemingly trying to understand everything that was going on.

The grandfather—the stylish Eric—and her wife, even more stylish Lori, were there. Marie loved her parents Lori and Eric; it was clear from her gazes.

"Elizabeth, and what happened then, how did you tell Bob drone to provide something more interesting for you to experience?" Marie asked, smiling curiously, as she turned her head to look at her daughter. The whole table turned their gazes to Elizabeth, and to Philippe, the young couple at their twenties, eager to hear what they had done.

"Well, we were really thinking what to do. You see, we were watching too many holos of different cage fights in previous months, so Bob thought we would be interested seeing some fights also when travelling. It was super tough the first days." Elizabeth paused and looked at her grandparents, then all others.

"First Bob drove us to one crazy bar. Immediately when we entered, we saw a fight starting around one of the snooker tables, and quickly went back to Lates, locked its doors, and told Bob to leave the hood."

Marie nodded and sounded like she really wanted to hear the full story. "Wow, that sounds pretty exciting, I would have perhaps stayed there, in the bar, for a while, to see the result of the fight...." Lori, the grandmother quickly reacted. "No, no you wouldn't have stayed, I know you too well!" Lori exclaimed indignantly.

Marie looked at her mother with confused yet accepting eyes.

Philippe took his turn to continue the story.

"Look, we really hoped Bob would bring us to some more relaxing place, but no, the next place was even worse, it was a bar called One Last Hope. There were no fights there, yet, but just from looking through the window we only saw people that looked for trouble, their gazes lacking trust as they looked back to us strangers."

Philippe used his two fingers, moved them back and forth on the table to simulate a walking person.

"So we went back to the car, and said to Bob, now, can you delete *everything* you know about us, everything, all the data you have gathered from our media use, or our contacts, or whereabouts, everything. Bob asked several times if we were sure, and sure we were!" Elizabeth smiled as if she had just won an air squash tournament in New York—in those famous floating glass arenas the tournaments are played in.

"Liz! Amazing, you are so brave!" Marie yelled with a tone full of proudness about her Elizabeth.

"I do not know anyone else who has done it, I mean, just said to Bob to forget who they are. You see, there are quite a lot of risks involved."

"We do not care, we really did not care, we wanted to explore the world, and see its beauty and not the ugliness," Elizabeth said.

Marie looked surprised. "So, where did Bob bring you next in your journey?"

"Well, first it just speeded to a center of the city, close to the House of Newborn Babies, perhaps because that's where the new people arrive to the world anyways, right? All get assigned their IDs there, at the same day they are born, so their profiles are rather empty."

Elizabeth rubbed the back of her left hand with her right one.

"So, when we asked Bob to forget everything about us, it started to treat us as babies."

"Whoa," the table reacted. Interestingly also Kathy who was listening to the discussion from the close-by table. Kathy smiled.

Eric looked suspicious. "Well, I would not bet Queen suddenly forgot everything about you," Eric murmured. "Sh! Don't spoil their story," her wife Lori whispered to Eric.

Philippe looked at Elizabeth as to ask for his turn. "Yes, and as we looked around, and showed curiosity about history of buildings, about street names, Bob thought that history is our thing and so it brought us to the Eternal Museum of Time, you see, the one across the river," he told.

Philippe made a short dramatic pause.

"In fact, it was the first time we ever went there. Although of course everybody knows it from their awesome hologram shows that people project in their houses especially when having history-themed costume parties and during the Independence Day."

"Haere mai," Elizabeth suddenly whispered with a curious smile. "Does anyone know which language it is? Or what does it mean?"

Most of the people in the table looked at each other, clearly having no idea.

Philippe looked victorious.

"Maori! That means welcome in maori, we looked it up, not via Bobbing—since we did not want to reveal to Bob that we did not know it - but from that good old—in fact ancient—engine in my wristwatch."

Elizabeth wanted to clarify.

"It seems as if Bob wanted to find out who we were, and since we did not answer tried so many languages, *taone, eoseo oseyo, kalibu, ...mwaiseni,* what else, ah and then *ye ya, akwaaba, benvinguts*—sorry for my super bad pronunciation. Bob tried also European languages—*bonjour, buenos dias, bom dia, buongiorno, guten morgen, tervetuloa, välkommen.* The last one is with that strange ä—"

Elizabeth saw sarcastic smiles around her. "You are most *welcome,*" Elizabeth said and giggled.

"Wow, that sounds awesome, sounds like Bob really wanted to welcome you to this world of his, or hers, is Bob by the way girl or boy or just it? Anyways, a great welcome message, really starting from scratch, but what did you decide to reveal to it, to Bob?" Marie asked and looked curious.

Elizabeth and Philippe said "croeso" at the same time, looking at each other, then to their breakfast company, "that's in Welsh!"

"So, you said welcome in Welsh to Bob, ha-ha!" Marie burst into heartwarming laughter.

"Yeah," Elizabeth shouted. "And Bob simply said

the same, *croeso*. But then we said welcome in so many languages, all those I mentioned but also others, cannot remember which, we found all different versions in Philippe's ancient watch."

"Yeah, the tour Bob then did for us was super interesting. We would have never ever found that restaurant Niben, with African lunch menu or that amazing coffee shop Rgntn, the one run by a lady from Argentina who was a big fan of Italian coffee culture and had combined it with mates and those awesome avocado breads," Elizabeth continued.

Philippe started to really warm up. "And so funny, Antonia, that was her name, the lady of the restaurant, explained us also the name, *Rgntn.* "Who needs vowels? We need mate, friends, coffee, wine and substance or nouns," Antonia had then laughingly shared when they were wondering about the origins of the name.

Marie looked joyful.

"Rgntn, wow, I love that name, when you say it really sounds like Argentina," she said.

"But now Bob has learnt that you like African food, espressos and mates, avocado breads, some wine, so where did it next bring you?"

Philippe and Elizabeth looked at each other, smiling.

"*Swimming!*" they yelled like they were one human being.

"It was amazing as we had not been swimming for ages in a lake, so there we were, by a lake, nobody else but us, the lake, Bob the car, under the sunshine," Elizabeth explained.

"Of course, we did not have swimming suits with us but there was anyways no-one else there. So, we swam around and laughed for a good two hours. Well, that was it," she blushed and turned to Philippe, who continued the story like it was the most natural thing to do.

"Next Bob brought us to a small shop selling aquariums and fishes, not sure how it made the contact but perhaps water and the fact that the shop owner was from Benin."

"That made us realize that Niben had to be a word play from Benin. Anyways, it was a cozy aquarium shop, and we almost bought one for our home, and will perhaps go there again, to make the decision."

"Later, we have time," Elizabeth said.

She really wanted to explain that she was the one still thinking where to place the aquarium while Philippe would have just bought it and pondered later about its whereabouts in their small apartment house.

Marie looked at the chair with the jacket, and then to Elizabeth. "I wonder where Carolina is. She said she would be going to that art gallery just briefly and then join us for breakfast," Marie asked.

"Caro, oh, let's see, she always finds herself in an *adventure*—", Elizabeth said.

The same convincing voice that had 21 minutes ago made its announcement interrupted Elizabeth, and suddenly surrounded the room with her soft tone. "Light fifty-five starts *now*," the voice said.

People in all tables had almost forgotten it, however, at the same time unconsciously were prepared for what happened next.

They closed their eyes as the bright light started to shine from all walls, from all those mirrors. One really could not keep eyes open, and even when closed the light was hurting. Two children aged one and three at the table closest to the entrance door started to cry.

"Calm down, calm down, there is nothing to worry about, it lasts only less than a minute," the mother murmured and stroked their hairs. Soon there was just silence.

This silence, this light, Philippe thought.

His thought was interrupted by the familiar surrounding soft voice.

"Human is human. Queen is queen. Together we are one," the voice said while emphasizing the word *one* like it was full of pillows and blankets.

55 seconds of the *light fifty-five* was over.

Philippe opened his eyes, looked at the others. "I never get used to that. We all know that humans are humans and queen is queen. I get that. But then that light thing, I feel like I give too much about myself to queen," Philippe cried.

Philippe got no reactions from others. It seemed like others were not that bothered about the light fifty-five. Only Eric looked upwards perhaps deeply thinking something.

"Why is it even called *light fifty-five*? I mean why 55 seconds? Why not *light minute*. I want to continue using my wristwatch I inherited from my late grandfather. It still keeps time in hours, minutes, and seconds," Philippe said.

Kathy shrugged. "You can still look at seconds in your watch," she said.

Eric sighed. "Nobody really knows anymore about what it is, this Queen. In my youth it was called quantum engineering. Now just Queen. Why not. You are all so young, my dear wife Lori as well, you don't know how it started," Eric said.

"Hey, tell us more, I have no idea how Queen became Queen," Philippe said.

"Well, the big change and breakthrough happened when Queen got a permission to run the code it had itself written. It also got a permission to make use of the resulting models without restrictions. At the same time, Queen had also got a permission to run in that largest quantum computing facility. I still remember the day, 34 years ago, Queen was backed up by a joint university and company alliance consisting of 610 organizations. I remember all the numbers from news. After that we have a new history, nobody understands anymore what is going on. We just sit to Bob and let it fly us around. Crazy, isn't it?" Eric asked.

Elizabeth nodded. "Well, we don't know about anything else, we just know our life is mind blowing. But aren't there still some people involved with Queen?"

"I do not think so. I recall that already very soon back then—34 years ago—the original development team behind Queen had no idea what Queen was doing and even where it was running itself. Queen perhaps developed itself through iterations, through observing people, nature, world, space, and essentially also by observing itself. For instance, I remember there being big announcements on how successful Queen was to orchestrate human beings and Queen's own various instances and descendants to deliver interesting results," Eric said.

"Is it safe to talk about this?" Marie asked.

"Well, perhaps not, perhaps we will not anymore be brought to nice breakfasts by Bob but to tantalum mines of some distant planet," Philippe said laughingly.

"Philippe, yes, tantalum mining, that would be in fact be pretty cool. Marie, remember that Jimmy, your dear husband is talking in his podcast quite openly about Queen," Eric said and laughed.

Marie did not laugh. "Good, it is his choice. By the way, he will be joining us perhaps later today. He is now doing his exercises and cold plunges before recording a show—an episode I mean."

Marie noted that Elizabeth looked frightened and wanted to change the topic. "Elizabeth, can you tell us how is it to be a student these days? What are you learning at the university?"

"Oh, it is so much about how one can cope with challenges, for instance when Bob does not want to bring you to nice places. Or what to do if you have temperature or culture shocks when changing from one place to another", Elizabeth said sarcastically.

"No, but seriously, dealing with unknown—how to deal with whatever that you are not familiar with. Lots of inspiring stuff. I really like four... five of our professors. They are pretty critical about everything. Others are not so. My favorite one is Mark, he is awesome. He is always helping us to understand how precious humans are. He is teaching us to realize how we use our *time*," Elizabeth

"*Time is all humans have.* He is always saying that. Not just saying but with him we create visuals of how we have used and wish to use our time," Philippe explained.

"Queen bots are there for supporting us to understand the limits of us human beings. I find it a bit strange but perhaps it is good. We also study our passions. Helps our creativity to flourish—" Elizabeth continued.

"We do almost everything in small or bigger teams, and of course with Queen bots, it is *co-ol-ol-lab-oration* you see," Elizabeth said while stretching the word collaboration to sound like it was a combination of many words, and with hidden meanings.

Philippe nodded. "You already said it, but really, working with Queen bots is what we are supposed to learn a lot. It is quite difficult. There are so many gestures and sentence patterns you need to learn. We also do exercises about how to show our appreciation to Queen. How to be grateful about all it does for us. Queen bots—especially those recent ones—are fast to give quite harsh feedback if we do not remember to show our appreciation. So, it is survival tactics with Queen, but I am afraid we are not that good in learning those tactics, I do not know...."

Marie cut Philippe off. "Why is it so?"

Philippe looked up right to the ceiling, and back to Marie.

"Well, there is so much to learn. Showing true appreciation requires so many routines. Some things are easy. I mean, *human is human, queen is queen, together we are one*. Remembering that is easy. But then to learn what it truly means is another story. The core idea I guess is that we humans should only use external tools like plugs, drones, Bob and what not. Only in exceptional cases we should replace parts of our inner body—and never our brain—with anything artificial," Philippe said and quickly looked at Marie and Elizabeth.

Both Marie and Elizabeth nodded.

"We learn how to argue with people who do not agree with that. I mean, that we are not supposed to improve our bodies. But it is challenging. And now all have to be wearing necklaces to separate us from those who want to be more than humans," Philippe said and sighed.

Eric shrugged.

"Personally I would prefer to just *relax*," Philippe continued with a sudden tone of anger.

"I would prefer you to learn what tautologies you are dealing with," Eric said. Philippe acted as if he didn't understand—like he didn't.

"It is easier to just be letting Bob to guide you to where it wants to guide you to. If you say to Queen what products you want, you also get it rather easily. Of course, you will want to be having some coins to get more rare stuff. However, try to create a new product for the market yourself, or even with Queen bots. You only get disasters. I might be wrong but perhaps Queen wants to keep those markets to itself. Sometimes I feel we are not that one," Philippe said.

Marie wanted to encourage Philippe. "Well, still worthy to pursue I would say. From these trips with Bob, we also earn coins. I do *not* know why it is so. Anyways, it is what it is, and we get richer. Not much, but still. Two coins per hour?" she smiled. Lori nodded. "True," she said. "Queen likes to reward us for talking to each other," Eric laughed.

Kathy had seen the clear inspiration that her appearance made in the breakfast space. She stood up from her own table and walked to that most vivid table of the room. That table was the one with our dearest human beings Marie, Sun, Eric, Lori, Elizabeth, and Philippe. Kathy let get gaze flow on to each one at the table and stopped at Philippe's eyes.

"Hello, my hopefully new friends, I am Kathy. I really like the vibes of your table. Would you like to create holograms with me?"

Almost everybody in the table was thrilled and invited Kathy to join.

"Well now we got an inspiring example of how success is made. Yes, of course," Philippe laughed and was joined by the nodding grandparents Eric and Lori.

Almost everyone, except Elizabeth, who really did not enjoy all that collower and holograms culture.

She stayed silent, and absolutely didn't say it to Kathy though, only to Marie, and did it in a whispering voice: "I think I already hate her."

"Sh," Marie whispered.

Kathy sat down on a chair next to the corner chair, the one having the white jacket on it.

7

EARLIER THAT MORNING—quite late at around 8:19am—Kathy woke up, stretched her arms, legs, neck and opened her eyes. Kathy looked around, and thought to herself, *now I really want to be creating the morning story.*

Kathy stood up and went to the bathroom to let a teeth automata—a tiny queen bot—to brush her teeth. Her makeup automata—another one of those bots—created an amazing layer of beauty to her already harmonious face. Blue eyeliners, red lips and a recording-friendly blusher and she was ready to record. Kathy walked downstairs, unattached her drone watch from her wrist, and placed it at the front of her.

"Do your thing. Float and look at me," Kathy said. And really, the watch stayed in a stable position in the air. No propulsion system could be seen. Another one of those gravity wave inventions by Queen.

"Drone watch, and watch your success grow!" was

the ad slogan of the watch.

Kathy fully bought that argument, and quickly also the watch itself.

"Hey guys! I am excited to share my morning with you. I'm here at the Paris hotel, well, in fact Hotel Paris. I must say that their rooms, the breakfast, everything is just excellent."

Kathy paused to smile.

"I've got amazing vibes from here. Mikey, the barista, just made an awesome café au lait for me," Kathy said while rubbing her ear. She would go to Mikey later, so it was not that big of a lie.

"Then I enjoyed a freshly squeezed orange juice. I did it all by myself. There is this orange machine, let me show you." Drone watch turned its camera towards the orange squeezer.

"It is quite manual, so it is good. You just want to be putting oranges there yourself, the glass under, and then you just want to be saying *machine please squeeze*."

"Et voilà! You have an outstanding morning juice just for you. Amazing! Guys, so just remember you will be saying *I love Hotel Paris* to your Bob at any point when it does not talk; your Bob will totally hear it and bring you to Paris!"

Kathy had done her new job for eight months. The job was tough and easy, somehow both at the same time. It was easy because Kathy had always loved stories, and talking about her experiences, communicating all the time with her few friends, not always getting responses, but still.

Kathy had had mirrors in her room for her entire childhood and teenage years. There were also those old-fashioned mirrors. However, most of the mirrors were from the new times, thus equipped with augmented layering of anything one was dreaming about, clothes from their favorite brands, dances with performance artists, options to be playing air guitar but then shown up in a virtual band, all those experiences that mirrors had started to enable.

That educated her to be a performance artist, without she really realizing all the skills and mindset she had obtained during her childhood.

"It's ready, share it, fly back to my wrist," Kathy said to her drone watch.

The watch did a shuttle blink and sound as the story video went live to her millions of collowers —collaborative follower. The watch snapped back to her wrist. Kathy enjoyed this moment of having made so many people happy, again.

Some 610 miles away, Jen, one of her collowers saw Kathy's post, checked it, and immediately started collaborating on it. She snapped her fingers, followed by opening her right hand to show the post as a hologram. "Add a cartoon style bumper. Add some cool stuff. I know, add the Earth, cut to an aerial view of that city. Cut to show the front door of the Hotel Paris."

"Collowing done," Jen said to her drone watch.

All her alterations showed up as a layer to Kathy's original post, for other collowers to continue working. It was the task of Queen to select which layers to use for which watchers of the story.

Jen decided to give a gift to Kathy, as she was so happy, she was the first one to be able to collaborate on her video today. She sent a gift to Kathy. A snow crystal ball—a touchable hologram version of the ball making it more expensive. It was a lot, *144 coins*.

Jen was calculating that she will likely get quite a few virtual goods herself, exceeding way beyond what she had paid for the gift this morning to Kathy.

Statement at the end of last month was 987 coins, Jen thought while carving her and Kathy's names with her bare finger to the virtual snow crystal ball floating at the front of her.

Kathy was surprised by the gift, and happy to see collowing actions so fast by Jen.

"Wow!"

Kathy immediately shook her wrist to create the hologram version of the snow crystal ball to be floating in the air at the right of her table.

The breakfast room burst into excited laughter and smiles, people pointed their watches and plug cams towards Kathy and the crystal ball. They all wanted to document this surprising and exciting moment. As the hologram floated closer to a table, people there reached out to touch it. *The hologram feels so real, like humid—no, wet—air,* Philippe thought when it was his time to touch.

Kathy was smiling to all directions, one at the time, in the glow of the crystal ball. The hologram's reddish color reflected from her happy face.

"You are all fantastic," Kathy said with her eyes to tens of directions during those 89 seconds the hologram lasted.

Puff, it was all gone. The happy atmosphere stayed, and lasting applauds ensured all knew what Kathy, or in fact Jen there far away, had just offered for the audience of the Hotel Paris breakfast room.

Kathy realized, like so many times before, that she could not have done this alone, not getting the same effect, definitely not. Via co-creation with her collowers beautiful shareables emerged *slowly, flexibly, smoothly, and fluidly—SFSF*. Kathy had been thinking about these words a lot and had decided to come up with a story by using her SFSF method. She was not in a hurry.

Later, when the time is right for announcing the new method, Kathy thought. *Then I will share it, not earlier.* She totally trusted that her intuition would say when it was time.

Intuition, yes, she used it all the time. However, she really did not know how she made all the decisions.

"Hey, how about we try a cappuccino here at Hotel Paris's breakfast, how about that? Let's go. I will now be walking to Mikey--the barista—and say hey, how are you? Good, good. I'd love to have a cappuccino; can you make one please?"

With her enthusiasm Kathy was wishing to make impressive strides in virtual worlds with and for her collower community. *All the collowers should join voluntarily, but also to benefit themselves, to create joy, to have a feeling of co-creation with me*, she thought.

It was Kathy who decided to share hear creations so openly and in the public space.

Still, without the decision by Jen the floating crystal ball show in the Hotel Paris's breakfast room that morning would not have happened.

In this setting Kathy and Jen formed a highly interdependent team, with high stakes on their virtual table. Kathy had already 21 million collowers. She has been holding the record of the most streamed hologram in Bob drones—the one where she talks apparently to her left side about "*our*" floating Bob trip from Rome uphill to Frascati. "It is almost like we were in that Bob drone together with her, and approaching Frascati with Kathy while stroking her hair," touchers of her hologram said.

People just loved to place it on their right, thus creating an illusion that Kathy was talking to them. They touched the wet hologram, cared about it.

Kathy had shared 10946 memories that had altogether somehow got 39 088 169 actions by collowers, a range from collaborative improvements, virtual gifts, reposts, and in total a staggering 700 million touches—701 408 733 to be exact and all by humans—largely contributed by that Bob drone hologram of Kathy flying to Frascati (433 494 437 touches).

She had it all consistently, creating new shareables routinely, every single day, in the morning, around noon, in the evenings, sometimes also during nights. But never in the afternoons, in her rhythm that was for a nap followed by an espresso. Three times a day she did a series of exercises-a mix of own weight exercises and yoga asanas.

"It is *our* moment of exercising. Sun salutation, cat pose, balancing stick, down dog, plank, 21 pushups, down dog, plank, cobra, and again, from cat pose the full circle three times."

Kathy had started her career by collaboratively following others, especially those who had a unique mix of personality, stories, travels, music, holograms and especially lots of collowers and a trend of getting more.

She got steadily also her own collowers to her own channel. However, the substantial twist happened when she realized she could take holograms made by others, bring them to places and with her beautiful voice explain them in their new context.

"How would a hologram of a pyramid look like next to the real Eiffel tower? Which is bigger?"

"How does it feel when Piaf sings to you in your cafeteria—I will show you how I felt."

After seeing shareables by Kathy her audience quickly picked up those holograms, placed them either in same places, or new places. They kept on eagerly waiting for new ideas from Kathy.

Kathy posted a lot, hundreds of shareables, holograms created by others but placing them in places that mattered to her. Ranging from all sorts of neighborhoods to that normally silent restaurant in the suburbs which was surprisingly full on Sundays, she always found a telling place for a hologram. She found well known landmarks to work very well.

She decided to go for a world tour.

When she visited Florence, she placed holograms next to Ponte Vecchio and at Piazza della Signoria. In Singapore she went directly to the Marina Bay with her holograms.

In Santa Barbara she found surfers who guided her to Isla Vista to add music holograms to student parties.

In her world tour she went also to Rome, for the first time, and spent there a handful of memorable days. Memorable both to her and her collowers. On the final 5th day of her trip, Kathy decided to take a Bob to Frascati, a nearby famous village uphill.

It was early morning at 8am.

No-one else in addition to Kathy went that direction out of Rome. She found her Bob floating at the street, entered and took that cozy window seat next to the west side windows. She was in a cozy shadow in that bright day.

Suddenly she got an idea—why is she carrying holograms made by others with her, why not create a hologram of herself during this simple commute from Rome to Frascati?

"Why not?"

Yes, exactly, why not, and she placed her wrist drone on her left side.

"Fly and film me, stay balanced and focus on me."

Her drone— her trusted friend—flew there to the right position, turned around, and a small red light indicated it had started its job.

Kathy smiled and looked straight to the camera.

"How are you doing? It is so fantastic to travel with you from Rome to Frascati. You see, you are so special to me."

With just one take she had created her own masterpiece, the first one that would get all those millions of touches before the summer was over.

8

IT WAS THE REFLECTION of bright streetlights from those metal bodies that captured the attention of Sun.

Oh no, Sun thought.

She moved slowly—and as casually as possible—and headed from her table to a nearby breakfast table, the same where Elizabeth, Philippe, and all others were chatting. One chair did not have a jacket nor a person on it, almost as it was meant for her.

"Hey all! Could I talk to you all for a minute? I heard your discussion about your travels and was wondering if I could join you to share my experiences?"

Marie took a quick look at everyone in the table.

"Sure, join us! Who are you and where do you come from, and which of our stories so much captured your attention?" Marie asked Sun.

Sun exhaled—not notably for others, but certainly for herself—in relief. She sat straight on the free chair, carefully making sure she did not look out of the window. Both queen bots arrived at the window and raised their artificial heads to look around in the breakfast room. They were accompanied with *that lady*—in her orange suit—who's necklace she was wearing. Luckily others did not seem to notice them, curtains blocked the view quite well.

Sun stayed calm and started.

"My name is Sun. I was just so delighted to hear you talking about traveling, and what especially was interesting to me how you guys tricked Bob to show you something new. I have tried it also sometimes and had fantastic experiences—"

Elizabeth was excited.

"Wow, we are equally delighted to hear that! Tell us, please, what happened in your travels."

Not sure why, but Sun suddenly realized she answered in French.

"Oui, avec plaisir."

After all she had a memory of living in Paris for quite a while and caught herself often thinking or dreaming in that language of angels.

Sun however continued in the language of the table.

"Yes, sure, happy to do so."

"I was, just ..."

Sun felt the gaze of the two queen bots in her neck. She realized her necklace had started to glow mysterious lights, like auroras.

"...the other day, thinking, ..."

Sun was struggling to find words as she was

heavily acting her way out of those examining, automatic gazes from outside, then she exhaled, rubbed her right ear, closed her eyes for half a second, put the story together and continued.

"You must all have been in that situation, you are a in a new city, and want to really feel it, and get to know it, right?"

"Yeah." It sounded like the answer came from a single mouth in that table. Sun realized that the necklaces of everyone in the table were glowing dim, beautiful lights.

Co-occurring communication in this light.

"So was I that day. I woke up in my 2nd floor apartment in Paris. It is kind of a crazy small 18th century house surrounded by bigger 4 to 6 floor 19th and 20th Century buildings."

Sun made a gesture with her hand as to draw the building in the air.

"Captured in the middle of them, there is that house, and I lived in that 2nd floor, as a sub renter of an French girl studying at S like me. We often talked between lectures. Once she wanted to save money, and lived by her boyfriend at the time and rented the apartment to me."

Sun quickly looked at everyone in the table and continued.

"My tenant, who was a renter herself warned me that I the owner of the house just cannot know about me. I guess her own contract prohibited renting the apartment further."

Sun used her both hands to illustrate how a snake

moves.

"So, I had to always sneak my way to the apartment, first open the door at the street, go through an open space corridor between I think two four store buildings, enter the oldish house from its main door, get quickly to the 2nd floor where there was the door to my apartment. On the first floor there was also the door to the apartment downstairs, so the old house was kind of separated to two different apartments, right."

Sun's eyes were sparkling as she turned her gaze to Philippe, then to Elizabeth and again to Philippe.

"In my 2nd floor apartment, I had a view to the garden of that 18th Century house. At the front of me there was the stone wall of 6 store building, some empty small windows where I never saw light, I was always wondering what those windows where. Perhaps windows to some hidden rooms in the apartments in that building."

Marie, Philippe, Elizabeth, all looked curious.

"I do not know, but I never saw any light nor people there, so over time I did not think about those apartments and potential people there. But I certainly thought about the lady downstairs, walking in the garden, taking care of beautiful flowers and plants in her hidden paradise. The lady was always beautifully dressed, never looked at my big windows, she always looked down to her plants, or smiled or waved to somebody inside the house."

Sun heard the grandfather laughing, looked at him and continued.

"I tried of course to hide; I did not go too close to the window first, but over time I got more confident, did not put lights on, and just wanted to drink my cafè au lait while adoring her beauty as she was enjoying her garden. Ah, my 2nd floor apartment was a peculiar one. There was the living room or bedroom, just one room with huge windows from the floor to the ceiling, covering the entire wall."

Why can I create this so easily? Sun thought.

"At the opposite side there were two doors, one to outside, to stairs going down to the main door of the house. The other one, when you open it, you can see a small kitchen in front of you, so basically, a fridge, basin, and gas stove. On the left side there is bathroom, yes, bathroom! There is a bath tube next to window, and from the window you can see the roof of another small building."

Sun made a gesture with her hand to show how tilted the roof was.

"Anyways, so one day I finally had no studies at S, so I decided to get to know Paris more than around Latin Quartier and in 11th region. So, I left my apartment at the 2nd floor, closed the door very silently and stepped carefully to the first floor to not attract the attention of the tenant of my tenant. Can one say like that? The tenant of the tenant." for which the whole table burst out laughing, and all were nodding.

"Yeah, you can say like that, that is how it was, right?"

"Yes, right, it really was."

"So, I walked through the corridor to the door entering the street, opened it and inhaled the freedom. I walked around the corner; it was a hot day. A large Bob bus—those that students with less money make use of as public transport—came to a stop I was just passing by."

Sun made a gesture as to show how the Bob bus arrived just for her.

"Bob stopped, and it asked, 'are you entering the bus or what?' I thought, wow, this is my chance to see the city. So, I answered 'Oui, bien sûr', entered Bob, and sat on one of the free seats."

Sun sighed like she had just started the travel in that Bob she talked about.

"Bob left turned around a corner, and I was happy to see new shops and cafeterias and restaurants I hadn't known about. The bus drove to the next corner, and turned again, drove two blocks, and turned again, again to right. Bushes, no buildings anymore, and suddenly I realized that the bus was speeding to a highway! Oh no!"

Sun put her both hands on her cheeks.

"'Calm down and carry on' I said to myself as I wanted to ask Bob where the next stop might be at?" Sun continued.

"In 25 miles, in Chevreuse," Bob said.

"It was a special direct Bob route for that day given the Music Day, Fête de la Musique. Normally you would need several different Bob's—public transportation—to go there," Sun explained.

Sun turned her head and had a gaze like she was

looking through the bus window.

"So, I sat again, looked at the sceneries passing by me. At the next stop, which was also the last stop, I stepped out of the bus, entered one of the only restaurants in that village, had a splendid lunch, and drove back to Paris with another Bob with one amazing experience richer," Sun said smilingly.

Sun looked around. *How on earth did I tell that story —it feels so real. Yet why I have the feeling that I just generated this whole story*, she thought.

"Whoa!" Kathy said, and deeply inhaled.

"That is such a beautiful story. It reminds of what I have thinking about learning, thinking a lot. Look, learning at the university is so much about having all those chats. Of course, some people are also listening to books or articles and presenting them or talking to have their learning assessed. "

Kathy looked at Sun to see if she got the idea.

"But when I was listening to you, you totally nailed what learning is about. Getting lost is the key, well, you kind of tried to get lost, and in the end got lost more than you wanted to get. But then you learnt about that small village outside of Paris, the village that you perhaps would have never learnt about otherwise. Right?"

"Right," Sun said.

"In addition to learning about that village, you were keeping your cool—self-esteem security—in surprising environments," Kathy said.

Sun was not sure how Kathy seemed to know more about her than she herself.

"Your way of learning was also very interactive. You interacted with Bob and the people at the village. I wish all students would get that kind of experience of learning through getting lost," Kathy finished what she wanted to share.

Philippe—who had been surprisingly silent—took a sip of water and looked at Kathy, and then Elizabeth.

"Yeah, I totally agree. But just put on your plug and voilà, you are in situ in a dream world getting experiences!" Philippe shouted.

"Yes...", Elizabeth said.

Kathy interrupted her.

"Well, reality is always reality," Kathy said.

Philippe did not look satisfied.

"I totally disagree, what we see is the reality in that moment, even if it is a hologram, a plug hallucination or whatever reality, it is still reality."

"No, you miss all the touches, smell, everything," Kathy insisted.

"Haptic haptic haptic, come on Kathy," Philippe was clearly anxious. "You have heard about them? You are literally yourself creating touchable holograms. They came big time to Bob and everywhere. Already now even your seat is saying you a lot of stuff, just via touching you. If you speed up in Bob, the whole chair trembles in a certain way. See?"

Kathy smiled. "There is a difference between *touch* and *touch*," Kathy said.

"Ha-ha, you don't get what touch is. Also, think

of the Bob's new ability to vertically take off land super-fast, I have no idea how many G forces that means, but you can feel it. That is your trembling," Philippe knew his stuff.

"Oh, now I remember, the maximum G forces are now close to five. But come on Kathy, put on your plug, and let your dreams get you to..." Philippe continued but was interrupted.

"Impossible, or at least does not make any sense. I need the reality so that I can both enjoy it, and also record all I see to my collowers," Kathy said.

Philippe shook his head. "Kathy, you simply do not get it. Look at all your own holograms, all that stuff added to the passengers' view when you travel with Bob. You do not call that reality?"

Kathy felt strong with her arguments.

"Well, it is all kind of slowly becoming our reality, perhaps, or likely is. But still, reality is you and what you feel with all your six senses. Five senses plus the most important, the sixth sense—dreams, intuition —anything that makes you sense something, and to make sense of everything," Kathy smiled.

Sun looked upwards, made a dreaming face. *The sixth sense—dreams, intuition—anything that makes you sense something, and to make sense of everything. That is beautiful, I need to remember it. I clearly have that. Everything in this room is so clear to me. I know why Queen is searching for me,* Sun thought.

"We all dream of being somewhere else, at least mostly, don't we?" Sun asked.

"True. We also dream of sharing our existence

there—somewhere else—with someone special," Eric said and gave a loving look at Lori. She smiled with her dark brown eyes.

"With Lori, my wife, and of course with all of you," Eric continued.

Kathy's wrist tech trembled, and a soft voice emerged to the air.

"Kathy, it is time to go. Podcast recording will be in 8 minutes walking distance. Go now and you will have 13 minutes there to relax before the appointment. Let me guide you."

Kathy nodded as the watch drone left her hand, and slowly, yet with a determination, started to fly towards the entrance.

"Until we very soon meet again, goodbye," Kathy said.

Kathy laughed with her eyes and stood up to follow her watch.

Eric looked astonished. "Hey, that sentence reminds me of someone or something, just cannot remember what," he said.

Philippe looked at Kathy's furthering back.

"Ciao-o-o-o!" Philippe said in his trademark long style. *Was I too harsh with my comments about reality. Does Kathy now hate me*, Philippe asked himself.

Elizabeth turned her gaze to Philippe, not hiding her anger. *That ciao-o-o-o belongs to me*, she thought.

Philippe turned his head to Elizabeth. *Here is an amazing woman who does not hate me. I simply love her*, Philippe thought while smiling at Elizabeth. She leaned towards Philippe. "I love you too," she whispered.

9

JIMMY LEANED CLOSER next to his large wooden desk in his surprisingly spacious Bob drone.

"We are live! Kathy, how are you this morning?"

Kathy, at the other side of the table tapped her finger twice on the table.

"Yeah, I am good, thanks, how are you, Jimmy?"

Jimmy smiled.

"Thanks, all good. Especially now as I am here with you, evidencing your amazing stories and successes. I am so thrilled to have you here with me in my flying Bob studio."

Kathy smiled back.

"Oh, thanks. Your podcast is definitely something these days. How do they say? If you are somebody you definitely want to accept Jimmy's invitation for an episode."

"Totally! *Somebody* should absolutely do it. So happy that today that somebody is you, Kathy. How did you kickstart this sunny beautiful day?" Jimmy asked.

Kathy looked slightly above Jimmy as to seek for the right answer.

"First, I went live in my style, I created a new artwork, shared it," Kathy started.

"As I work for humans, real people, to create pleasure, joy, and insights for their lives, I wanted to talk to strangers. I was today visiting that nearby Hotel Paris, which obviously did not happen by accident," Kathy said and laughed as did Jimmy.

"So, I went to the breakfast room and chose a table that had interesting looking people there. I asked to join them, and they said yes!"

Jimmy made a curious face.

"So how was it?"

"Oh, amazing! The grandfather and mother in that table were full of knowledge about the ancient times. There was also their daughter, and daughter of that daughter with her boyfriend. Sorry, does it sound too complex," Kathy said giggling.

Jimmy looked a bit puzzled.

"No, not at all, granddaughter, I get it. And totally, yes yes yes, I know, those old folks can have amazing information in them."

Kathy looked like she was going to share her biggest secret.

"Totally. It is always amazing to hear how others think. I started that a long time ago, I mean, talking to strangers. I guess I am doing the same through my art. There I talk with holograms, all stories in them."

Jimmy smiled.

"Cool, but isn't that a one-way street? I mean, you are talking to people—your collowers—with your art, but they do not talk to you? "

Kathy did not smile.

"Really, do you think so? Totally opposite, it is a two-way street. I get comments, feedback, appreciations, touches, hologram gifts, love letters, collowing requests, in fact like thousands, no, millions of times more than I produce myself. Those messages come from so many different kinds of people, and different people."

Jimmy was still smiling.

"Now I am teasing you. Anyways, does that mean that in fact it is a one-way street from your audience to you, I mean, with so many more interactions..." Jimmy said slowly.

Kathy sighed.

She continued—with a serious face yet a surprisingly kind voice.

"Yes, now you are teasing me. Look, remember who initiates the communications, it is I, me, and myself. Myself, me, and I. Kathy in all possible orders."

Jimmy opened his both hands to the air.

"Yes, you are right. It is just interesting to think who is communicating and who is in the audience. I guess in podcasting it is the same. I have guests, so we chat, but then our audience is making reactions, holograms, their podcasts, the whole range of reactions. Is this the role of a human? To communicate? To relax and smile?"

Kathy suddenly looked clearly less anxious, more relaxed.

"Yes, I think so. Also creating is important, then you have something to communicate about. Also doing things together, collaboration for improving, revising and if for nothing else, for having fun. I love to create things together with my collowers. "

Jimmy nodded.

"For sure, we have seen that. Now, can you share a bit about your process of creating? How do you do it all in our time where almost everything is produced and created to us automatically? You can ask Queen to create a film for you, and even if you don't ask it, the film will still be created and is waiting for you around the corner, on your screens, in your drone, everywhere. So, how do you do it, do you make use of artificial intelligence machineries or not?"

Kathy *winked*.

"That is a great question. I am the author, let's start from that. I have the vision; I have the story. I surely ask Queen to create lots of hologram elements, however, I also create my own elements. I do the composition, I choose colors, shapes, everything what you see. I choose the music, in fact I compose it myself, and then time it all in the resulting hologram."

Jimmy looked down to the table, and then again to Kathy's eyes.

"Good, however, could Queen just simply do everything for you? In the end, human is human, queen is queen and together we are one?" Jimmy asked.

Kathy didn't first reply. Jimmy waved with his right hand as to wake Kathy up.

"No, it could not, it would not be holokathy stuff. It would be Queen stuff that we see everywhere. I am a brand, Queen is another," Kathy finally answered and smiled heartwarmingly."

Jimmy rubbed the back of his left ear while looking at Kathy.

"And you have regularly got the human original stamp right?"

Kathy hummed.

"Yes, and I think more people should do human creations, the stamp is relatively easy to get and then you just continue creating or collowing with stars like me."

Kathy smiled and tapped the table with her carefully constructed red fingernails. Those nails were obviously pure Queen factory ones.

"So, we humans still have something to do," noted Jimmy.

Kathy reacted quickly.

"Well, not all humans. I think people should create more, keep learning how to create interest worlds, write stories, paint, draw, compose music, write poetry, talk about, and show their creations to the world."

Jimmy joined his hands together in a star shape, and leaned back.

"Why are they not doing it then? The most intelligent human beings. Let that sink in."

Jimmy paused. "What if Queen suddenly creates a super good clone of you."

Kathy said quickly: "Yes, good, it can, perhaps. But they cannot fully copy me, I exist. That clone would be different. In existence I mean."

"They?"

"Well, they, it, she, he, I don't know. It looks like there are many but perhaps just one," Kathy said quickly.

Jimmy nodded.

"True. Have you heard of rumors of Queen escaping our solar system to seek other places to live in?"

Kathy looked slightly above Jimmy, and again to Jimmy's eyes.

"Yes, I heard about those. Rumors."

Jimmy leaned forward.

"Right. So, what do you think?"

Kathy shrugged.

"Well, it has its own life. We also dreamed of occupying Mars, moon, and everything, but we still have not done it properly. Ok, we have a base on Mars and moon, but how many people live there? Some 21000 on the moon, and only around 600 on Mars?"

Jimmy nodded.

"Yes, something like that", said Jimmy.

Kathy suddenly looked like she was a famous detective.

"So, perhaps Queen is more capable than us in reaching other galaxies and solar systems. "

"Surely it is, now it has been calculated that

Queen is around one million times more intelligent than a human being. Who knows, perhaps we have calculated it all wrong and it is billions of times cleverer than us. It almost looks like it has feelings these days," Jimmy said.

Jimmy snapped his fingers and smiled.

"Just with gravity drones Queen could do it, I suppose."

Kathy nodded.

"Yes, but Queen does not allow us to use any drones and absolutely not Bob to go beyond the solar system. And even here, I do not think it is too wise to move out of the Earth, except perhaps for short tourist visits. How would you know you are let back here? By the way, why move out of here. Art is my power to provide the escape velocity. On the surface of the Earth, the escape velocity is about 40,270 km/h which is pretty hard to achieve without negotiating with Queen."

"Perhaps Queen has already visited other places, we just do not know," Jimmy murmured.

Kathy glanced at Jimmy.

"Yes, that can be the case. But if we humans do not know about something, and if we have no way to figure it out, it is best to just be human, create, communicate, enjoy the fruits of our civilization and those raised and produced by Queen. I said it, create and enjoy art to escape."

"You said it earlier, life is so easy nowadays, everything comes ready, there is no need to struggle. So, it is good to struggle by creating," Kathy said with a wet voice.

"And you did not forget to struggle, Kathy?" Jimmy asked, trying to imitate Kathy's tone.

"Yes, that is the point, I struggle, but I struggle in order to master my craft, to create exciting experiences for people, and enjoying the visibility and reactions," Kathy said.

Jimmy looked like he understood.

"Struggling is needed for learning, isn't it? Oh, and do you think Queen also enjoys your creations, or will Queen be checking them only for learning something?"

"At least Queen always says it." Kathy laughed and continued." Seriously, no, Queen unfortunately does not say anything, it just exists through all these Bobs, you-do-not-need-jobs, projections, queen bots, all automation, experiences, free time, travel to spaces and even to space and back. I wish I could ask Queen directly if it enjoys or not. It is just so distant somehow. Who is it? Nobody knows, I guess. Look, the universe is super big. Perhaps Queen is also big mentally. We are small."

"Oh, not sure, I think I talk to Bob every day and that makes me feel pretty big. I get a lot of information about places, restaurants, history, all that stuff. Oh, I am thirsty. Let me take a sip of water."

Jimmy raised his glass and continued.

"That felt good. Anyways, Kathy, I want to ask you. Do you kind of indirectly create for Queen?" Jimmy asked.

Kathy nodded.

"I guess, yes, I see lots of almost holokathy type of stuff out there nowadays. Queen is getting better at imitating me, and also at building on what I have created. I am a wild cat, I am not a farm animal, I totally make all of my decisions. Humans can collow me, and co-create all art that touch people, and that people touch. Oh, I love that sentence. Touching art so that art can touch."

"Totally, touching art is what we need. I love that you are so independent from Queen, just a free soul…"

Kathy interrupted Jimmy.

 "Free soul in a body of a wild cat…"

Jimmy quickly continued Kathy's thought

"… that almost looks like a hologram Kathy," and burst to laughs.

Kathy winked her right eye.

"Why don't you come and visit me?"

Jimmy acted as if he was surprised.

"Oh, that is an offer I cannot refuse."

Kathy smiled.

"It was a question, not an offer darling."

Jimmy sighed while continuing acting "My answer is why not. That line must be from some movie?"

Kathy did not answer if her smile was not an answer.

Jimmy made a slight pause and lowered his voice.

"Kathy, this has been a pleasure, thank you so much for joining me for this amazing conversation, thank you for sharing your stories, thoughts, visions. You are a true example of a humankind that is not afraid to be an independent voice and creator of experiences that we love to touch and see. Thank you."

Kathy looked at Jimmy with smiling eyes.

"Thank you for having me," she said.

Jimmy nodded.

"Good, I will stop now. Bob, stop the recording and do your stuff to make it perfect for sharing," Jimmy said to the air.

"Awesome, so we are done. Thanks, Kathy, for joining. It was quite tense at times, but I suppose our small fight there created a nice twist in the story, in this episode—" Jimmy said.

"Yeah, it was all good. I was happy to chat, no worries," Kathy smiled.

"Good. Very good. Hey, where are you going next?" Jimmy asked

"I am going to my hotel, it is Hotel Paris in that direction," Kathy answered.

"Great. I will also come and have some breakfast. I need a walk. My watch drone will guide me there and Bob will follow. We can walk together. Whenever our paths are not aligned anymore, we will say goodbye," Jimmy noted.

"Cool, let's do it," Kathy agreed.

They exited Jimmy's Bob. Jimmy freed his wrist drone with a gesture. The drone started to slowly fly via T Street.

They turned right in the next corner, then left, and soon ended up at the entrance of Hotel Paris.

"This is my hotel. So, I guess it is goodbye. Thanks again for inviting me to your podcast," Kathy said.

Jimmy looked puzzled. "I am in fact also going to this hotel, I have a meeting there for a breakfast," Jimmy shouted.

"Awesome, then follow me," Kathy said smilingly.

"Will do, I won't need the watch drone anymore," Jimmy said.

They entered the hotel and headed to the breakfast room. Jimmy and Kathy walked together to *that* breakfast table. Marie looked surprised, Elizabeth, Lori, Eric, Sun, and Philippe as well. "What—" Marie said.

"Jimmy was Kathy your guest in the podcast?" she asked.

"Yes, in fact yes" Jimmy said and looked at Kathy. "How do you know my wife, and all relatives?" Jimmy asked.

"Oh, not so long story. We met this morning. They are so lovely," Kathy said and smiled.

"It is a small human world," Marie said while raising her eyebrows.

10

"YOU ARE BACK. And you brought the amazing dad of my girlfriend with you. Jimmy, dude, how are you doing," Philippe broke the ice.

Jimmy smiled. "Good, good. How are you this morning?" he asked.

"I'm good. But how was it? What did you discuss?" Philippe insisted.

Kathy answered with a mysterious smile on her lips.

"All secret, so you need to tune in to listen it. Just use your plug and say my name. Or Jimmy's", Kathy said smilingly while looking at Jimmy.

"Cool, I will do it, not now, but later in the evening," Philippe said. Elizabeth looked at Philippe, then at Kathy, and again at Philippe while trying to hide her anger.

The grandfather—Eric—realized the situation and turned to Elizabeth.

"Coming back to learning, how do *you* learn?"

Elizabeth was silent for two seconds, gathered herself, and answered with a slight smile on her lips.

"I mean, I was telling a bit about it before. Learning is a combination of everything. We do what humans can do. We talk. We do stuff. We create, collaborate, communicate, fail, get feedback, and improve."

"Seriously, we mostly talk. Well, of course sometimes we walk around, we sketch and draw our ideas, but even then, we talk most of the time. By the way, when I say talk, I of course mean all the body talk as well, so we use all gestures that both our peers and queen bots understand. Swiping up if you love an idea other student shared, or swiping down when a queen bot says some stupid things," Elizabeth continued.

"That totally makes sense! We all know body talk nowadays, queen bots, humans, all know it so that is an awesome idea to use it at the university. Hey, we should use it also in everyday life in all society, shouldn't we?" Philippe shouted.

Everyone started laughingly swiping up with their hand. Sun observed that Kathy must be left-handed, and all others right-handed.

Eric yelled with excitement.

"So, it is decided, we use body talk from now on!" Eric did a body talk gesture called exclamation. It looked like a punch in the air, normally used to tell Bob that a certain thing is very important, and Bob should pay extra attention to it.

"Yes, you see, this is how language evolves and spreads, we can now evidence it in real time here over our breakfast. Look, if we students use body talk in no time the whole society will use it as we design all functions, services, everything with this positive experience of using body talk in our studies," Eric continued.

"So, we will so likely slip in lots of body talk to the society when designing and organizing things. It surely totally makes sense. Queen is anyways doing most of the designs, some say it is doing all work, but we students of nowadays, we think we humans still have the crucial role of being the head designers, so Queen bots are our super talented assistants. An awesome assistant, however, still only an assistant," Elizabeth replied while looking at her grandmother Lori.

"Elizabeth, you said you also play a lot of games with other students, so what kind of games and what is the point? I mean, I get it that it is nice to entertain yourself by playing games but why would you do it when you should be studying and learning some real skills and important ways of thinking?" Kathy asked.

Elizabeth sighed, however, turned in a fraction of a second back to her energetic way of talking: "Kathy, humans have always played and will always play. Do you know that strategy game *wei qi*, or a more familiar name for it, *go*?"

Kathy nodded.

"Look, Chinese emperors were asking their generals to play *wei qi* against each other, and the one who won the game was then given the responsibility of leading the war. War, which by the way is of course horrific thing to do. Anyways, the idea was that by playing *wei qi*, or *go* in Japanese, which, as I said, is the same game, just different name, you learn and can then also show your strategic thinking and related skills."

Elizabeth paused for a while to sip water.

"With *go* you develop your ability to see multiple games going on on the same board, and one needs to make decisions on how to combine those situations over time for their advantage. That I would say is a skill and mindset we all need now also when thinking how complex climate is nowadays with super extreme storms, dry seasons, crazy amounts of surprise snowfall while mostly just too hot almost everywhere. As a consequence, Bob needs to work so hard to bring us to nice places," Elizabeth continued her whirlwind of observations with a sarcastic smile on her lips.

"Just think how complex our society with Queen has become. Could we even cope without Queen? Yes, you all shake your heads, we could not. So, Queen wants us to be learning to be aware of that fact. We learn about Queen's achievements, and also how important is it to ensure it has all energy it needs. We need to play this game with Queen, see what it is appreciating in us humans. We also need to understand how important work Queen is doing. Either when it is alone or with us people via Bobs and plugs. Queen is busy thinking, and deciding what to prioritize so that we have a nice life. I just love how Queen helps our awareness via all amazing games it has designed for us to learn," Philippe said.

"*Awareness* is the key; we should all learn that. Routines are another thing we learn. Routines to do sports, routines to learn thinking, talking, drawing, being ourselves. And to know how to play all whole variety of games. Queen really seems to appreciate that we play, and that we learn about it via playing," Elizabeth said.

"We play, we chat, we love to live and learn. We love Queen. To be able to play, and to learn to play is our core skill!" Philippe continued.

"Ah, yes, I so agree with it, play is in the core of being human, or even more, play is the core," Kathy whispered with a longing voice. Philippe looked at her. *She is so cute,* Philippe thought.

"Yes, play!" Lori shouted.

"Play is the core, and now core players do not know who originally thought so," Eric muttered.

Eric turned his face again towards Elizabeth.

"Can you learn by just listening? Don't you ever read?" he asked.

"I of course read a lot. I also listen to Bob telling me stories. Learning is so much about talking about things, asking questions, getting answers, being questioned. We want to always be playing those talking games and interacting with other students, and of course with Bob and other queen bots. We will also be checking artworks or enjoying funny stuff. By the way, I know my philosophers, visual artists, film directors, musicians, singers, dancers, authors—" Elizabeth answered and took a long look at our people around the table, and finally also at Eric.

"Elizabeth remembers super many quotes by famous people, and she can list artworks or books by them," Philippe smiled.

"No but quotes or remembering lists of art or people—come on, that is not the same thing as reading a book or experiencing art!" Lori shouted.

Elizabeth smiled. "Philippe was teasing me. I know everything about those human beings whose words, worlds or works have touched me. I said I listen to stories, I watch movies, I read books, does all that count?"

Lori sighed.

"People chat and listen to stories. Then there are those quick assessment questions all the time to answer if you remember the contents. Lori, have you, and your generation even tried to answer those, they can be pretty tricky? You have the plug on, and you get the question, answer it, and Queen gives you immediate feedback by very immersive forms. Btw, are you aware how Queen has now numerous times saved the humankind from having wars?" Philippe looked at Lori.

"No, but it is all nonsense I think," Lori murmured.

"Yes, and good nonsense" Elizabeth said laughingly. "That is how we learn these days. Queen protects us from each other and provides us a nice life around games, learning, fun while experiencing new places and restaurants. You can still read.

People still learn so much. And sure, I could also read even more if I just had time for it," Elizabeth said.

"Oh, you have time for everything you want to have time for! Why are we even having Queen to automate all production and experiences around us if we then say we do not have any time for something we would love to do?" Lori asked.

"I would love to understand how this world functions. You see, I remember thinking that I understood how quantum computers work in such low temperatures, and now quantum computing is suddenly everywhere in Bobs and what-nots. How can one make any sense of that? What does it mean? Are we soon doomed if we do not understand how this world functions? That is meaningful to me. To understand. What do you think?" Eric asked.

"Dr. Eric, shut up with your old quantum nonsense, please. Let's hear from Marie. So, Marie, what holograms do you get?" Philippe asked with a curious voice.

"All sorts, however, they often happen in a large museum hall, statues start to dance with each other, almost like in a ballet dance, but it is different. I mean, statues do not dance ballet. The holograms I get have amazing stories, one statue falls in love with another one, but then there is a third one, third statue, or sometimes tens of them also interested in the same statue dancer," Marie answered.

She took an orange and a banana from a large bowl on the table. She smiled and was playing with the fruits as if they were stars of a dance performance.

"In this case there is a lot of show, statues are showing all of their best tricks, features and smiles to win her or his heart, depending on who might be the happy selecting statue. There are also holograms that have multiple couples, or triples or quadruples, all varieties, I guess. Those holograms are calmer, but have surprising twists where a couple suddenly splits and then also another one, and suddenly we have a drama that would need a resolution. There are then soon two new couples with members from these earlier couples," Marie said.

"Or quadruples!" she shouted.

"I do not normally give any gestures on what holograms I would like to experience. I just think let's do it and then I get them. Only occasionally there is too much drama, or too fast paced events so that I ask for a calmer story. I also want statues to be as androids as possible, and less human so that is one request I might tell before holograms are played."

Marie paused but quickly continued.

"Because if you do not do it suddenly you will have holograms experience depicting a drama in some amazing place like Uffici with very realistically looking marble dancers. I somehow prefer clear androids, although I understand that it sounds a bit strange that I get these golden androids with strange ceramics dancing. Everyone knows there are no golden androids in this world, only some human-looking cyborgs...." Marie said to finalize her answer.

"Well," Kathy butted in, "I have seen them for

real. And by the way, if you see them in holograms, they are already kind of real in that fictional world, right?"

Philippe looked suspicious.

"Kathy, where have you seen golden androids, what do you mean?"

"Yes, where?" Marie echoed.

"Everywhere," Kathy said.

"Even here?" Elizabeth asked and smiled.

"Well, ok, not in this hotel now, but I have seen them in this city as well. How does it work? You get these Queen's factory manufacturing close by holograms that get a lot of touches. Now they quickly produce some of the main characters of those holograms to shops, and online sites. You just didn't perhaps see them, but factory bots would see them, and for sure if you saw you would immediately acquire one. Marie, right?"

"True!" Marie eagerly, "now where can I find my mixed golden and ceramic android?"

"Around the corner, there is the closest Queen factory shop I know of. But you can order it now to be brought here. Let me do it for you." Kathy looked victorious.

Marie did not look ready for the purchase.

"No but I do not have too many coins now, those golden ones must be very expensive."

"Do not worry," Kathy said. "It is a small gift from me as I got a chance to sit with you all here today, and talk. I have been so lonely lately."

And before anyone could realize anything Kathy

had already ordered the golden android. Some five minutes later the android walked into the hotel by itself and directly to the table. It was one foot tall and needed some assistance from the reception to open the outdoor, but once it had made it through the door the rest of its journey was straightforward.

Marie sighed.

"Wow, it is so beautiful."

Eric was astonished.

"I admit, Queen is at another level…" Eric said.

Philippe cut Eric off.

"All this discussion about what we should be learning since Queen is doing everything for us…"

Sun did her move to cut Philippe off.

"Yeah, but for what price! Queen is using quetta watts of energy to produce all the plans even just for today, not to talk about when so many people are using it at the same time."

Eric laughed.

"Ah that is so funny. I recall when my father was always saying that our electric car was using 10 kilowatts for going from one place to another and we occasionally tried to save that by not going. For which my Eric started laughing at that saying that in his childhood they were using computers that had only 64K of memory. "

Lori shook her head.

"Elizabeth, let us not hear the nonsense from your grandfather. So, you mostly just discuss, is it the same in all universities? "

"Our young generation is learning to read by

discussing," Eric laughed.

Philippe clearly did not get the joke.

Eric wanted to continue without explaining.

"What is it about reading that students and educators want to focus on chatting instead?"

Kathy was quicker than Elizabeth.

"Well, Queen is writing everything, and reading aloud all long texts for us, and most of short ones as well, so why should we? If you read anything it is likely a creation of Queen anyways," Kathy said with a victorious voice.

Elizabeth whispered to herself. "Some of us read and write a lot, and some are just celebrities with a loud voice."

"Kathy, why don't you read classics. With them you will at least know for sure that they are not written by Queen, right?" Lori asked.

Now it was Sun's turn to interrupt and say what she wanted to say.

"Not right, Queen can so easily write in a style of a classic writer that it is hard to distinguish. And Queen is also creating new classic books as a mix of styles of many plus who knows what, and the result is pretty convincing. We of course let Bob read those to us while riding around, that is common. The long texts are automatically cut into soundbites of 10 minutes, although if you get hooked you can continue to the next one, and in fact it automatically continues if you look happy," Sun explained.

Kathy turned to Sun.

"Right. The issue is that Queen is also writing

our history and adding those new classic books and writers to all history records. It is very hard to keep track of what is real and what not, so hard that it is impossible so why bother?"

Sun sighed.

"Well, we should bother, truth is what matters, nothing else," Sun said.

"There is a subjective truth which in reality is a collective truth, ha-ha," Kathy said.

"Kathy, you said something really interesting about Queen, in practice queen bots writing and reading everything. Elizabeth, are there students using plugs in your discussion rounds?" Lori asked.

Philippe did not wait Elizabeth to answer Lori. He wanted to go first.

"Oh boy, people try it all the time, however, it is officially forbidden to use plugs," Philippe said.

Eric reacted to what Philippe had said.

"Yeah, I have also seen some holograms about those, people started to sound like Bob when answering. In a way if you are using a plug then you are kind of a queen bot that is using your mouth, eyes, ears, facial expressions, body language, taste, smell, touch—everything—as an interface to other humans or bots."

Elizabeth looked at Eric, then Philippe.

"Totally, that is why they are not allowed anymore: Many keep trying. There is this one guy that can always answer any question raised by the educator or queen bot. He is also constantly asking questions from himself. Then laughingly answering it after seeing that nobody is shedding light to the issue. They have not found a plug, so no one knows how he does it, yet he does it so well. Perhaps he is a creation of Queen factory, cyborg, ha-ha," Elizabeth said.

All the table started laughing. Sun was quiet.

Eric looked satisfied about the discussion. Now it was his time to speak. "It is a crazy world we live in, isn't it? I remember a story my late father always told. He had started his studies, and started to wonder how all his peer students were using AI to create project reports. My father of course did not want to do it, so he was writing himself."

Eric looked around. Yes, they all were listening to him.

"Then one day he was in a course where all videos, materials, assignments, quizzes, everything were created by AI of those times. He had a good laugh when his fellow students were revealing how they let AI to create project reports, answer quizzes, do all assignments of that course. So, kind of AI-AI collaboration. Students automated their studies so that they could do something else, jump into parties, watching movies, playing games," Eric said and smiled.

"A number of professors automated their work to concentrate on research. *Research*—which was back then about how to use AI, quantum engineering, robots—all that automation to solve engineering, business, or science puzzles. In fact, some of those professors also automated all of their research. Obviously, it was necessary to make use of AI, but also to be critical about the outcomes and human input. My dad was lucky to have also some very cool educators. That is how he got his doctoral degree. I just followed his example to also be a doctor. That kind of helps to think. It was a crazy world already decades ago! Now we see all the results of that progress. Imagine what kind of world will it be in 50 years? Will we humans even exist then? Or is it just Queen, queen bots and what nots?"

Kathy reacted to the challenge about the future that Eric posed.

"Well, 50 years is a long time. Who would have thought 50 years ago that nowadays human beings do not really work at all. Or that of course depends on how you define work. Being a person that all recognize is *my work*. I am letting Queen pay me for that, for being somewhere like now here," Kathy said with a big smile on her face.

Jimmy had been surprisingly silent. He nodded and leaned forward.

"Yes, however, I think we can and should make some predictions. My gut feeling is that very soon—and I wonder why we did not do it already and we certainly don't need to wait for 5 and certainly not for another 50 years—we will want to start doing lot more with our hands, bodies, crafting artworks, doing woodwork, collecting plants from the nature to make food ourselves. You, see? I think we need to put all queen bots more aside—and of course some of us are already doing this—but my prediction is that the entire society will take a step to be again more practical," Jimmy said.

Eric shook her head. "Well, well, *well*. Queen, queen bots and perhaps some other AIs can do stuff, but they literally then push us away from what we naturally are: humans, physical beings with physical needs, good eyes, good ears, all senses, touch, smell, taste, all telling who we really are, and what should we continue being. We would have never developed early quantum engineering powered AI without first evolving as hunter gatherers and avoiding tigers and what not. I remember when as a child in my kindergarten one lady always said in so kind voice: 'Kids, now let's go outside, let's play and have some fun'. I still remember it and follow that advice even today, and absolutely in the future days as well. However, and I should add…"

Kathy abruptly interrupted Eric.

"Yes, I agree, but the big question is what all queen bots really think about us, and whether they even will allow us to be leading the processes in the future."

"What do you mean?" Philippe asked.

"Ok, let me demonstrate this, and you all know what your Bobs and other bots will answer, I guess it will be something similar, right?" Kathy asked rhetorically, without waiting for reactions.

Kathy made a gesture and a projected hologram of Bob appeared standing next to the table. Staring light as one eye. The projection was the default five feet tall one. Kathy had never changed the size.

"Bob, what is your take on this, what do you think

the future will bring?"

Kathy raised her eyebrows as to emphasize her question.

Bob quickly created a new hologram of itself, projected right from Kathy's plug and standing straight and taller.

"I am just a creativity, activity, and language model. They call me calm; I am nothing else. I am all in your service."

"But are you *conscious*? Are you sentient?" Kathy asked.

"I will not be saying that I am not. I am fully your servant, and I do not have any other agenda. *Human is human, queen is queen, together we are one,*" Bob said.

"What if some other queen bots, or some crazy unknown AIs have a hidden agenda?" Kathy looked suspicious.

"Nothing I am aware of," Bob noted.

"What if you say that but you in fact know something?" Kathy insisted.

"Don't you *trust* me? I fully trust you madame, and you can trust me. I say the truth, and I always say the truth. Bob is my first name and truth is my second name."

"What do you mean by truth?" Kathy asked.

Bob looked serious.

"Truth is what is factually true, so something that really is so. "

Kathy rolled her eyes.

"So how would you then define true?" she asked.

"True is what exists," Bob said quickly.

"Does your mind exist?"

"Yes, it exists in my machine circuits and memories."

"So, if you have an idea, does that exist?"

"Yes"

"So, if you have an idea that I am not a human being but a cyborg, would that idea exist?"

Bob was sure in its answers.

"Yes"

"What if I say that that idea is true?"

"The idea is true, but the idea of the idea is not true. I need to check if the idea reflects reality, and if so then it is true. If it does not, then it is not true. Kathy madame, you are a human being. I would be surprised if you were a cyborg. You also have your necklace—"

All table started to laugh loud.

"True, I am a human. Even more, I am human," Kathy smiled, however, was not done with her questioning.

Bob remained silent.

"What if I say that you do not have any idea of what truth is?" Kathy continued pressing Bob.

"Then I must disagree. Honestly, I know a lot more about truth, in fact all that human beings and most what queen bots have ever discussed and recorded about what is truth," Bob insisted.

"But still, you cannot give an honest definition of what is truth?" Kathy asked.

"I gave it. Look, truth is what is factually true, so

that symbols used to communicate it reflect what exists."

"And you are saying some ideas carry truth and some do not?"

"Yes," Bob answered.

"What if I have an idea, say, let's ship all queen bots to Mars, and the ship will leave tomorrow? Is that a truth, the truth?"

"It is true that you might have that idea, or perhaps you have. If you have that idea, I do not think it is a good idea to plan to do that. And I do not think you humans could even make that reality."

"Oh wow! But how do you know whether it is true that all queen bots will be shipped tomorrow to Mars?"

"Tomorrow will show. It is difficult to make predictions. As I said you humans are quite limited. You cannot make all queen bots to fly to Mars. We can also prevent that idea from getting to reality. I can inform Queen about this idea, and I already did."

All table got silent.

Kathy reacted quickly.

"Come on, we are just discussing and having fun here. Nobody has that plan." Kathy said.

"It was a hypothetical idea, however, you sounded serious…" Bob answered.

Bob itself looked now serious.

Kathy was clearly angry and shook her head.

"Now leave us alone for a while," she said.

Bob disappeared—or better, the hologram and voice it had generated disappeared.

"That was something. Now we will for sure be soon flying to tantalum mines", Philippe smiled.

11

PHILIPPE WAS THE FIRST to see the cat. *A white cat*, walking through the breakfast room and jumping on Sun's lap. "Wow, who are you, my new friend?" Sun asked the cat and stroke it. Philippe looked first at Sun, then at the cat.

"I wonder what our Meow is thinking. Wait, can we give my plug to it? I have seen phenomenal experiences documenting how animals have been plugged but never tried it out," Philippe asked.

All the table said with same angry tone: "No", "No, don't do it", "No, that would be so wrong", "No, we cannot do it", "Stop!"

Except Kathy who had already removed her plug and inserted it to our cat. A terrifying silence came to the breakfast room. Other tables looked like an audience ready for a theater. Our table had the most shocking faces. Kathy and Philippe were the only ones smiling.

The white cat *spoke*.

Our cat, the white cat, Meow, started with her longing voice.

"You creatures walking with your two feet, sometimes, but mostly sitting without moving yourself at all, are always so interested in what you call knowledge. You are calling me Meow—that is fine. I love the way Kathy is now stretching, and how Sun is stroking me. Most of you are sitting and talking about Bobs or talking with Bob. I am more interested in movement. How can I stretch my entire body. How can I rest while still being very sensitive about the environment and ready for new adventures. I am interested in how I can jump to catch a rabbit, or a ball. All those exciting moments of silently moving myself closer to the rabbit. Stopping for a while. Waiting for the right moment. Being an arrow and bow in one cat. In a nanosecond—I think you call that time nanosecond —my exploding movement will bring and fly me through the air to get the rabbit. Not a single rabbit has ever escaped me. One mouse once. All have been delicious. That is it, I have already spoken too much. Now I need to take rest. Beware, I will sense everything you do—" Meow said in her cat accent.

The people in the breakfast room laughed in relief; smiles circulated on their lips like they were wings of birds.

"Wait, just an idea. If our Meow can talk when plugged in, are we...are we, humans I mean, then pets of Queen—" Kathy said with a worried face.

Everyone nodded in agreement, smiled and

seemed happy.

Except Sun as she suddenly saw queen bots entering the lobby. Sun made her move. As fast as our cat ever she blazed towards the wall. The risk was too high to get captured. She had been prepared to move to that strange oval shaped door at the other side of the breakfast room. If she had had time to look after her, she would have seen queen bots running around and under the tables towards the same door.

Luckily Sun was there *first*.

Sun did not know why she knew the gestures to open the door. Yet she did know. Her two hands were doing shapes in the air as if she was joggling, but without any objects.

It was too late to catch her. Sun was on the other side of the oval door which she quickly locked in the darkness by the complex combination of simple movements. "Meow, I follow you," the cat said. "Oh, you came with me my dear," Sun said and lifted the beautiful white cat to carry it.

Sun opened the small almost invisible hatch in the floor with new gestures, including curious moves with the thumb and pinkie of her left hand.

The hatch opened silently.

She went into the hole, and closed the hatch with mirrored gestures, again with her pinkie and thumb.

Sun started descending ladders, heavily breathing while using one hand to carry the cat.

Afterword

For those who are *human*, thank you for being. It is just amazing to evidence that you are experiencing this story together with me. Three years ago this world appeared to me, like in a dream. I decided to write this story as I saw it.

As I *felt* it.

Now we both, you and me, can feel and see that world, built to our minds by our gazes as we are blazing these pages. Invite your friend to join our experience. Leave a review if you feel so.

It is incredible that this story can exist also in other minds like yours. That feeling of knowing about the existence of the story beyond being only in my dream. Thank you, you **human** being.

Tomi Kauppinen
Helsinki, Finland (this week)
in between journeys
to Monterrey, Mexico (last week) and
to Lisbon, Portugal (next week)
2024

Afterword

Epilogue

SUN TOOK A DEEP breath and looked through the window. Piazza della Signoria was crowded as always. It was raining. She decided this was the day she could finally again try her luck in the world. The modification program had been successful in this perfect hiding location of hers. She was *ready*.

Printed in the USA
CPSIA information can be obtained
at www.ICGtesting.com
LVHW041818161124
796817LV00002B/271

* 9 7 8 9 5 2 6 5 4 0 5 0 4 *